BATHWATER

VICKY FOSTER

BATHWATER
Vicky Foster

ISBN 978-1-903110-65-2

First published in this edition 2019 by Wrecking Ball Press.

Cover design by humandesign.co.uk

Many thanks to Arts Council England,
BBC Radio Drama North, Sue Roberts,
Shane Rhodes & Louise Wallwein.

Bathwater

Scene 1

Jos: 1st January 2017
The day my life changed ... well, it was night actually. When my life
changed, I was sleeping. I used to have this blanket that I always
took to bed; it was blue fleece. Real soft. And this night, I had it in
bed. And course, I was asleep. 'Cause I always used to sleep alright
with that blanket. And so everything that happened happened while
I was warm and cosy at home. And I didn't know anything about it.
Funny that, innit? How your life can change, and at the time, you
don't even know. And it was like my anchor, that blanket. You could
use it like a pair of arms, giving you a cuddle. It was like safety. And
it smelled like toast. It used to smell like toast.

Vicky: It's January 1999, in Hull. In an ex-council house, now private
house, a two-mile drive from where I grew up. I've just dropped out
of college, for the second time. I'm 19.
His palms are pressed against mine.
Calloused and strong, they pulse with promises;
bass-lines to stories he whispers, trawling the air above us.
They echo through plaster, rafters and brick,
shake the sky, so that light spills down
in lines; illuminates his words.
We are transfixed by the glow
of the future we're drawing out
in these biting black empty rooms.
We lie on the living room floor.
No mattress. No bulbs.
Walls hold off rain, but not the cold.
We protect ourselves from the January freeze;
these words, low gas, body heat.

Jos: I wish I knew where it began.
The seconds, the heartbeats that change everything.

Vicky: He was my New Year's Day.
Smiling face an open question.
Whole lifetimes playing out across his palms.
I was his New Year's wish.
Barmaid in his local pub. But not to him.
To him I was a princess. And he would drink my bathwater.
'Come out with me,' he said.
I took his hand. A shiver
worked its way along fingers and up our forearms.
A too-hot curry. A pint too many.
And then a kiss. A rush of wind.
Footsteps on cobbles to bring us back to earth.
Our bubble is formed from laughter.
People in the supermarket stop to tell us:
only real love will sound like that amongst the packets and tins.
His car carried me here,
to bare walls where I sketch and draw.
We packed my old life away in the loft.
It brims up there with discarded papers and poems;
most populated place in the house.
We will fill the rest. Ground up. Together.
He knows how it's done. Has learned to slip his tether.

Jos: I wonder how you make a man.
I wish I knew where it began.

Vicky: His shell is crafted from hard work.
Spirals of pulling against. Away from
a past that would hold him under,
he's swum so far against the tide.

And now I will help.
We'll shine light in new rooms. We begin
by sanding to bare plaster. Then paint. Long nights. Extra coats.
For a man who spent months in a tin can underwater,
this is luxury. For a girl who thought
she would never be wanted, this is luxury.
We scratch our names in the old brick.
Etch promises that scatter orange dust
and fade beneath our brushes.
We scratch out a new life
in emulsion and cheap carpets. Buy a bed.
Fit pipes that pump hot water.
Plumb the toilet and the bath. We breathe it to life.

Jos: His hands have stacked wood and worked it to flame.
Passed exams that earned a uniform.
Lashed on breathing apparatus,
held maps, checked hydrants, broke down burning doors.

Vicky: And now he holds me. Lashes me firmly
to a new life that will withstand storms.
We will find a peaceful breeze.
And then, I become a pea-pod. There is sprouting
in me. There is growth. There are two blue lines
on a plastic stick. And we will be three.

Jos: I wonder when they first held me

Vicky: We stand beneath an arch beside the sea,
the wind swirls up inside of me, and I greet the son I know
is coming. Our linked fingers already shield him.
We open up a room that has not yet seen paint.
He prises open Polyfilla, pastes the contents

over cracks and bumps. Sands out imperfections.
And I swell.
I am ripe and growing.
I am a bellyful of arms and legs.
A new person, about to begin.
Half me and half him.

Scene 2

Jos: 15th January 2017

My mum's got boxes and boxes of stuff up in the loft – but she won't let me in there. Sometimes she'll bring down some of my baby stuff; my first baby-grow, the little tag thing you have on your arm when you're born, some photos. Like she'll only let me see the things she wants me to see. And I reckon she's saved every pair of shoes I ever owned. OK, maybe not every pair, but all the ones from when I was little. Maybe that's just what mums do...

Vicky: January 2000. I'm 20, and Joseph is a four-day-old miracle.
This warm water is his womb now.
Comforting and threatening at once.
We hold him. My gentle hands.
His rough, awkward in this
soft act of

Both: support.

Vicky: We pass a flannel cloth
between us; fibres full with soft suds.
We soap down every limb, every inch of
newborn skin, marvelling at the realness
of him.
We don't speak now of hopes or plans.

These grew with

Both: the bones of this boy

Vicky: resolved into solidity

Jos: vertebra, femur, fibula,
calcified foundations,

Both: feet firmly held.

Vicky: His fingers grasp too tightly at fatherhood -

Jos: no dad has modelled the softness required of knuckles and wrist

Vicky: but he will learn.

Jos: There must be a way to learn, to grow.

Vicky: Night feeds have proved more testing than night shifts.
The patience required to placate a rooting mouth,
slips from him in sleeplessness.
But he will learn.
These cells that blossomed into my boy were split,
multiplied, inside of me.

Both: The seed of personality, pressed into fertility.

Vicky: And I fed him – kale and cabbage and rich red steak.
I grew him strong.
He was born with long fingernails.
Long dark lashes that lay like butterflies at my breast.

Both: We wait

Vicky: for them

Both: to take flight.

Vicky: Reveal the world to waking eyes.
I whispered promises as he heard his first night.

Jos: The dad who would carry me home...

Vicky: I breathed oaths to maternity room walls.
Foam rivulets run over his face.
He threatens a cry. A hand
that's almost too quick rocks his head.
Not quite enough to startle.
Joseph's calmness is coaxed by our hands.
His trembling lips a hangover from the shock
of nakedness. I have soothed him with warm words,
hushed tones. Trust me now. I'm here.
Suddenly red blooms in the bathwater.
Blood. Surely blood.
Joseph arcs his mouth into a scream
under my panicked hands.
I raise him up. Check for the source.
Behind me glass shatters on tiles.
This is not blood.
It is Tom's red wine.
He is in a rage.
His eyes are fists.
I read his lips over Joseph's screams.
He storms through slamming door.

Jos: Who would hold me?

Vicky. I see the ruined water.
Cradle my

Both: shaking child

Vicky: against my chest.
I wonder what this means.
So soon after bringing Joseph home.
I remember

Both: whispers I've heard,

Vicky: whispers of Tom's dark past.
But I push them away. Think about the new stories
we'll make. Think about fresh starts,

Both: what love can do for a person. What it can heal.

Vicky: I think about his

Both: wish. For me. For a family. A home.

Vicky: I know it'll be OK.
Joseph has stopped crying.
He's safe and warm in his towel.
I carry him through to his new room.
Gently dress and lay him on flannel sheets,
press his blanket into place around him.
I go back to the bathroom,
watch as the brindled water
runs away, swirling into darkness.

I rinse the stained bath, replace the plug.

Let it fill.

Scene 3

Jos: 1st February 2017

When I was a real little kid, I used to love my little men. Used to take them everywhere – wrap them up in little bits of towels and fabric. I always wanted to keep them safe. Used to tuck them in at night. I remember once I lost them in the supermarket. My mum said I cried my eyes out, so she went back in and asked at the desk, to see if she could get them back....

Vicky: January 2002. I'm 22 now and Joseph is a smiling two-year-old bundle of energy.

I love it here. It's one of my favourite places. And I know that's sad. But there you go. I love Asda, what can I say? Usually I come on my own. Just me and Joseph. That's how I like it best, if I'm honest. But what am I meant to say when he offers to drive me? Wish he hadn't bothered though. He's been in a right mood since we got here. Joseph loves it. I think he loves the carrot sticks really. Healthiest two-year-old I know. Me and him, we love our carrot sticks and hummus. I just need to grab some fabric conditioner and we're nearly done. I wanna get clean bedding on tonight so we're nice and cosy. I wish I could tell him that – but he's being so grumpy. Like he doesn't want to be here. I don't know why he came. To be honest, it feels like I don't know what goes on in his head a lot of the time.

Tom has things that crawl along his veins at night;

wake him empty eyed, blanched knuckles,

spite spilling onto bedsheets,

bruising walls.

And I don't know what to do when that happens.

They don't sell stuff in here to clean that up.
But it doesn't stop me trying.
Some nights he'll get a phone call,
disappear for hours. If I try to stop him,
his body is a brick wall.
He'll come in, skin scented with smoke,
unfamiliar fingers.
Won't answer questions.
Not anymore. Not since I freaked out
about the things he told me he had been doing.
I wish I could catch hold of him,
slow him down, make him see
how he looks to me.

Both: Some things are irreplaceable;

Vicky: the sunlight over

Both: his shoulders

Vicky: when I wake. Feel

Both: his breath

Vicky: against my back. The shared smile at Joseph's waking words.

Jos: My footsteps, headed across the landing, trailing fingers along the walls, singing.

Vicky: We are intricate, filigree, porcelain, held in the fretwork web of our joined fingers, but his hands are starting to slip.
So right now, I'm

Both: holding

Vicky: on for both of us. I'm

Both: pulling

Vicky: with all my might
to steady Tom's hands against the

Both: fragile weight.

Vicky: But he's bigger than me.
He's stronger.
If he pulls or pushes hard enough I'm worried

Both: we might all break.

Vicky: But I breathe it away.
I pray that I'm strong enough for this.
The old ladies that we meet here
seem to know this feeling as they stop at the trolley –
tell me what a beautiful son I've got,
what a lucky lady I am,
how not many men would be here
in the supermarket on a Wednesday morning.
I see the crisscross of veins and wrinkles
running like rivers over their hands.
I know the stories about how it's the women
who really hold things together.
And I'm trying. I am trying.
Suddenly hands are 'round my throat.
Back shoved against tins.
Fist eyes. Furious face. His

Both: lips are moving

Vicky: but it's

Both: like a bad dream.

Vicky: He lets go. Steps away

Both: like nothing's happened.

Vicky: I look around. The aisle is empty, thank God. Joseph cries. I pick him up, soothe him. Stroke his back. Tom has stormed away, out of the aisle, and I wonder how I'm gonna get the shopping home. Push down the panic in my chest. What just happened? He must be tired. That's it. He's just tired. Been on nights. God knows the sights he must see sometimes at work. It must be that.
He's coming back down the aisle, and it doesn't look alright at all.
He chucks a roll of black bin bags into the trolley.
I don't know what you're saying.
Why would you put your stuff in bin bags?
You can't. You can't do that.
What about Joseph?
I look at the stuff in the trolley.
The stuff to get us through.
The stuff to eat, to clean the bathroom.
I don't know what to do.
And my hands are shaking, on the handle of the trolley.

Both: I can't cry.

Vicky: Not with Joseph looking at me.
There's nothing else for it.
I'll have to go and find him.

Take him home. Fill his bags.
Watch as he leaves us both behind.
And if I'm honest I'm scared
what he'll do without me holding on
but maybe things will be easier for us when

Both: he's gone.

Scene 4

Jos: 3rd March 2017

I've still got my blue blanket. But I don't use it anymore. One day, I came home from school, and my mum had washed it, and it wasn't the same anymore. It smelled like fabric conditioner instead. And I know she meant well, but it didn't work anymore after that. So, I just keep it in a box under my bed now. With the photos. The ones from before that night. Before my life changed.

Vicky: It's October 2002. Joseph is three in a few months. Surprisingly we're doing OK. Toddler groups, friends, things are OK. I keep him in toys and Clarks shoes. But a knock at my door has brought footprints all across my clean floors. Not black boots. Not just policemen. These are detectives. And they've got questions. Just when I thought I'd got us settled, got me and Joseph sorted, got cleaned up.

Jos: I'd have been all tucked up. Toys piled neatly in a corner while I slept.

Vicky: 3 months.
He left 3 months ago.
Erm, sometimes.
Sometimes, yeah.

I don't know if violent's the right word.

Not to me.

Well, other people.

People who pissed him off.

I'm not really sure.

Why are you asking?

Jos: And I wish I hadn't asked.

Both: Almost wish I hadn't questioned.
There's a woman in a car park.

Vicky: Well, they found her in a car park. Nearly dead. Red light district.

Jos: And someone's said it's him.

Vicky: Someone's said it's him, and suddenly my mouth is a leaking tap.

Both: My head is spinning with things he's done

Vicky: and my mouth? My mouth is a leaking tap...
I tell 'em about you screaming at an old lady in the street. I tell about you bundling a man naked into a car, threatening him. I tell about you strangling your uncle. How I pulled you off. About the bottles of vodka. The smashing windows. The story you told me about a hammer in someone's eyes. A hammer in your hand. I tell. I tell about you saying you want to kill me. I tell them about your hands around my throat. You saying it'd be better if I was dead. You saying you'll kill me one day. And now there's a woman in a hospital. Scarred for life. And they think you did it. I think you did it.
They bring panic alarms. Red buttons. Cameras in my windows. And sign the statement.
My mouth has leaked twenty-five pages of things you've done.

Both: But nothing about the cool of ice-cream against lips and throat in the heat of a summer garden.

Jos: Not that time you saved a little girl in a house fire. Laid her back against cold night pavement to bring her breath back.

Vicky: Nothing about that man with emphysema who said you saved his life with letters and phone calls and a shiny new machine in his living room. We had cups of tea there once.
You say, 'I know what you've done, bitch.' You say, 'Heavy wind can break phone lines.'

Both: Your face in the paper. Your face in the news. Everyone knows.

Vicky: Eyes slide over me in the nursery playground, at the corner shop, in the street. I visit you once. Bring Joseph. They told me I shouldn't lie. That I should tell him the truth.

Jos: What does a three-year-old know of prison? I'll tell you what he knows. Harry Potter. Azkaban. And then night terrors. My Daddy in a haunted castle.

Vicky: I bring him. You are shrunken and sickly. Your eyes dart about like bluebottles looking for an open window. And I know you've done it. I know then. And they've got you banged to rights, they tell me, but

Both: doubt is a prison cell.

Vicky: CCTV footage resembles the defendant, but is poor quality.
Blood is present on shoes, clothing, and car belonging to the defendant.
Samples are deteriorated by cleaning products, and are incomplete.
The defendant was known to frequent the red light district. This

could explain the transfer of blood onto clothing and shoes.

Both: He was a fireman

Vicky: at the time the attack took place.

Both: He says he did not commit this cowardly act.

Vicky: The jury

Both: cannot decide

Vicky: beyond a reasonable doubt that the defendant is guilty. The defendant can now be sentenced for the assaults on two previous victims, for which he has already been found guilty. The defendant has served his time in custody, and is free to go.

Scene 5

Jos: 4th April 2017

Bath times are brilliant when you're a kid, aren't they? We used to have all these daft songs we'd sing – there was one for washing your armpits to, one for washing your hair, and one for afterwards when you were getting dry. We'd sing them real loud. Top of our voices. But I can't even think about that anymore. Don't know if I'm remembering it right or not...

Vicky: January 2005.

He was back again tonight, banging on the windows while I tried to distract Joseph in the bath, hoping running water and daft songs would drown out the noise. I didn't call the police this time. They never do anything anyway. Two years of phone calls, of collecting video footage of him, on my path, where he shouldn't be. And nothing they can do. Last week they told me we might have to move away. New town. New names. No chance. I'm not doing it. We won't stand a chance. Not the way I am now. I can hardly leave the house. The sky's too big, you see. Daft, eh? But it is. The sky's too big nowadays.

Too much possibility in all that space.

Both: All my boundaries have crumbled

Vicky: in a flood of new information.
I'm choking on muddy water,
on his filthy fucking bathwater.
It fills my face and nose, takes my breath.
I can't breathe out there.

Jos: I need something solid.

Vicky: Need something to hold onto.

Both: All my stories are gone.

Vicky: I just have facts.
Half facts, counter facts. Grainy video footage.

Both: Nothing to hold onto.

Vicky: The sight of other men's hands, lowering a child into a buggy

Jos: The sight of other men's hands, crooked to lift hair
out of smiling eyes

Both: is a physical pain.

Jos: I need clean white walls to block it out.

Vicky: I need four walls to block it out

Jos: but sometimes white paint hides dark secrets.

Vicky: These walls have secrets.
I know what's underneath that white paint.
I see it. Everyone sees it now. My name, his name, Joseph's name.

Jos: Words scratched in dirty brick.

Vicky: Sometimes I think if I could scrub hard enough, I could scrub them out.
But I need them. Need these walls between me and
all those eyes. And hands. Hands that could curve
around objects.

Jos: Hands curved around a sharp object.

Vicky: Hands around a blunt object, that could curve around my throat.
The sky is too flimsy. Particles of air. No defence. And when my back's turned, how do I know what's happening? Seconds...

Both: can fracture everything.

Vicky: And time, fractured, stretches infinitely; there's too much in it.

Both: Too much possibility.

Vicky: And anyway, I just stay in now. Try and keep the house clean. Try and keep it clean, after all the footprints. Because you see, I stay in, but people don't stay away. Him. Every week. On my path. So then, police every week. Walking around, looking at everything. Eyes on all my stuff. People wanting to talk. A waste of time, 'cause I can't open my mouth. What might come leaking out?

And then, today, social services came too. With a piece of paper for me to sign. Saying I won't let him see Joseph. And they might as well say that I can't be trusted. Who could trust a woman who would trust a man like that? And so I'd better sign this contract telling me what I can and can't do with my own kid. As though I hadn't been back and forth to court all this time, telling them that he shouldn't see them. Suppose at least someone's doing something though. Someone's saying something's not right, at least. I signed her piece of paper. Made a promise. Not one I'd ever thought I'd need to make.

Both: It's not the kind of thing you hope for, is it?

Vicky: I've been reading this book. I've been reading a lot. Not much else to do once the floors are scrubbed and Joseph's at school. I've been reading about magic and quests and wizards and karma and, well, this book was about Wicca. About re-directing energy. About how, if someone's doing bad things to you, and it's getting you down, you can just redirect the energy back at them. And so I thought, yeah. Too fucking right. That seems to fit the bill. Getting me down is one way to put it.

And I've tried everything else. And I feel a bit daft now, but fuck it. I thought I'd give this a go. I'm sick of being fucking quiet. So, whatever he's sending on me, I send it back on him. Right back in his fucking face.

Scene 6

Jos: 29th April 2017

I loved primary school. I remember my first day - feeling real smart in my new school uniform, new school shoes, new bag. There was a toy fire engine in my classroom. I always wanted to play with it, and the teacher always used to make sure I'd get it at play times. She was nice like that. I think I must have been her favourite. And I remember my mum, smiling.

Vicky: September 2005
I drop Joseph at the classroom door every morning.

Jos: I remember her dropping me off. Waving from the classroom door.

Vicky: My hands are deep inside my pockets, but my arms – my arms are holding off the sky. They are painting sunshine into his days.

Jos: I remember sunny days. I didn't see the shadows then.

Vicky: I will not let him grow in the shadow of this. I wave goodbye, get into my car and try to stop my hands from shaking. My organs, my limbs, my bones, they ache with the impact. And with trying to build a new life. I don't suppose this is normal. It's just the nearest I'm going to get. There are certain places I can't go – car parks and streets where pain is condensed. Where I can't look away. If I stay away from those places, I'm nearly OK. Nearly, but not quite. Driving's the hardest. Driving and the supermarket.
There's a tic in my brain, a short circuit that jumps in unexpected ways.
Slides dark snapshots in amongst the shopping lists,
the place that works the pushing of pedals,
how the gears shift.

Both: You build up walls, but blood has a way of seeping through.

Vicky: Who knows why these things billow and balloon the way they do?
Like the movement of red liquid dropped in clear water.

It threatens as stains at the corners of your happy photos,
and you do not let it in.
You store them in a sunny place. Dry.
Away from floods.
But still, the supermarket's hard. I'm gonna get through it though.
I've come this far. Worst part was getting past the newspapers on
the way in, and I've done that. Tom's face is still the front page.
Tom's face and the faces of the people who did it.

Both: Hammers

Vicky: in their hands this time.

Both: Hammers

Vicky: in his face.
Violent end for violent man.
Vicious revenge killing

Jos: Violent end for violent man.
Vicious revenge killing.

Vicky: But I can't be thinking about that now. I need this shopping for
Joseph's teas. For his pack-ups and breakfasts and suppers.
My heart's hammering hard. Air round my head is light. Floating
away. Everything too bright. Wanna close my eyes, lay down here in
the aisle with the tins of tuna and wake up normal.
Everyone says Tom's dead. But not to me.

Both: See him everywhere.

Vicky: His face is sometimes in between the tins. His eyes stare out at me
from the dark.

Jos: In my bedroom at night.

Vicky: In my bedroom. Or the bathroom. Especially the bathroom.
Heart hammering hard. Air round my head is light.
Shame is not a prison cell. It's more like a soundproofed room;
people hand down sentences like antidotes and words bounce off
and back at you on repeat. My son has

Both: lost

Vicky: his

Both: father.

Vicky: He's better off without him. My son's

Both: father

Vicky: has been

Both: murdered.

Vicky: He brought it on himself.
All these words, inside this room, with nowhere to go.

Jos: Nowhere to go.

Vicky: And you get in a big space like this supermarket – and they just have
further to dance, and they're like a

Both: cacophony

Vicky: that only you can hear. And other people think these words should cancel each other out. But they don't. Negative plus negative does not make positive. It makes an equation that my mind can't contain, it's stuck in a loop

Both: wearing down my brain.

Vicky: People are starting to look at me, and I'm not sure if it's 'cause they know or whether it's 'cause I'm muttering to myself and blocking the aisle. But either way, it's not good. Think they're getting to know me here now. Probably sick of loading all the stuff from my abandoned trolley back on the shelves. Last week it wasn't the tinned fish aisle that freaked me out – sometimes it's fresh meat; sometimes I get all the way to the freezer aisle – that's worst. Trolley full of all the things I need to be a good mum.

Jos: Need my mum.

Both: Need hot chocolates with marshmallows, carrot sticks, soft vanilla buns.

Vicky: Actually, getting to the freezer aisle's not worst. Worst is getting through all the aisles and leaving the trolley at the checkout. It's easier to explain – check bag; forgotten purse. Rush off. Usually the people on the till are nice - sometimes a bit grumpy – but always they say they'll keep it there til I come back. I never come back. Those days it's chippy for tea and whatever the corner shop's got in for pack-ups. But today is not gonna be one of those days. Today is a good day. Today I'm getting round. I'm soothing myself. Soothing all these thoughts away. I've been talking at last. Not so scared of my mouth anymore. Clearing my lungs of all the shit they've sucked in. And it feels good.
I'll tell you what's gonna feel even better though. Putting all this stuff away when I get home.

Scene 7

Jos. 1st June 2017

She's never told me about that night. She thinks I'm too young. But I'm not daft. I know all about it. She thinks I don't, but I do. The kids at school don't let me forget it, 'cause they all know about it too. So why does she think I wouldn't? She thinks I'm daft. And there's loads of questions I want to ask. But I can't 'cause if I start talking about it, I can see her lip shaking. But I still wanna know. Like, do I walk like him? Do I talk like him? Is my body the same shape? I'm nearly grown now. So she must know …

Vicky: June 2017

Joseph's fist is dripping blood
onto the cream carpet.
I'm watching his feet.
Hoping he's not going to step
on the broken glass.
Son, it's OK. It's OK.
You're not a bad person.
Don't say that.
It's never too late,
especially not at 17.
Never mind what you've done.
It doesn't matter.
What he's done is put his fist
through the TV.
Shatter the Sunday morning peace.
Hurl obscenities at the walls.
At me.
Thirteen years have taught him
that his grief doesn't fit
inside the box of other people's everyday.

There's no place for it in school.
Rage bubbles out of him,
unbidden, when he should be doing maths.
The words he repeats to me
are the ones the voices in his head
repeat to him.

Both: Google is a bad dream I can't wake up from.

Vicky: I'd packed secrets away in the loft,
waiting for the right time.
But Google has been flaunting them
behind my back, all along.
He's grown too tall now for me to hold off the sky.
His legs have outrun me.
His fingers have found their way to headlines
I'd hoped could wait for years yet.
And it's all crashed down on him.
All in one go.
He tells me he aches to feel.

Jos: The gristle of another man's ear
between my teeth.
I ache to make fists, to find release in another man's face.

Both: Sometimes, instead, fists find the wall.
Sometimes, instead, head finds the wall.

Jos: Sometimes, instead, I'll take a pill,
smoke some weed.

Vicky: He'll scream at the world.

Both: Run away.

Vicky. I phone the mental health team.
Social services. The police.
I pack away sharp objects in safe places.
And the footprints find their way
all across my clean floors again.

Jos: Soft hands bring me home.
Sit me down. Press my chest.

Both: We crack our ribs.

Vicky: Show them the pulsing darkness there.

Both: And hope they can help.
Really hope they can help

Vicky: To tame these things.

Both: These are not dead things.

Vicky: They do not lie still.

Both: They growl and screech.
They scratch and nip.
They do not lie still.

Vicky: I've seen what they can do to a person.
And I need that not to happen now.
The density of blood has never troubled me.
I know it like the back of my hand.
Like the back of Joseph's hand.

Like the inside of his hand,

where it pulses,

half-him, and half-me.

I know what Joseph thinks that means.

I want to bend reality for him.

I want the one where we eat ice-creams in the park,

with his dad. The one that meets me some mornings

behind the screen of my eyelids.

But as I start to open them,

there is melting, there is dripping,

it doesn't stand up to daylight.

Joseph, it's OK, son. It's OK.

Scene 8

Jos: 1st October 2017

They say these voices in my head are anxiety. Probably all these unanswered questions bouncing around and off each other. That's what I feel like I'm doing sometimes, bouncing around. Bouncing off walls. It's like somebody's taken my anchor away, and now I'm just floating about. There's too much space. Too much not knowing. And I don't know what to do. Don't know how to make it stop.

Vicky: January 2018

My face is pressed

against the white washed wood

of the bathroom door.

Inches away,

beyond my sight,

Joseph holds a sharp object to his face.

Jos: Clean-edged steel. Scar-scattered arms.

Vicky: I ache to steady his hand,
arc a curve, show the way.

Jos: Need to steady my hand,
need an arc to lean into.
I need bass, running water.

Both: Don't know how to begin to...

Vicky: Days in the steam
sharing suds together
are long gone now.
And I'm on the other side
of the bathroom door,
worrying over the smooth, soft skin
that's now beyond my reach.
I can't shake the feeling
that You-Tube is no way
for a boy to learn shaving.
But this has been his teacher,
and now his first practical session.

Jos: My face in the mirror. The blade in my hand.
Go steady. A fresh start. A clean shave.

Vicky: The pounding of bass reaches my ears
over running water. A dull low voice,
and Joseph's, raised in a fast-paced beat
that I can't decipher.
He's in time
with his music,
that I don't understand.
I know I'm safe

in an otherwise empty house,
to whisper promises against the wood.
Hope they'll somehow find
their way into his fingers,
into his brain.

Both: I send out wishes
and hope
and oaths ...

Vicky: I know you've felt the cool glance
of splayed weed fingers at your ankles
know them from the fringes of your childhood dreams.
They picked at your pillow edge as you slept.
You might be tempted to follow crooked digits,
let the pull of the past like an undertow tug you downwards,
to turn dark rocks like treasure troves,
test your palms against their smooth solidity.
You won't breathe there long though.
You have always been heliotropic.

Both: You do not have to grow where you land.

Vicky: I will cradle you.
Wrap your tender, growing bones
in pastel shades of love.
Pick them clean.
Wipe them free
of worry and anger.
Soap you up
in iridescent foam.
Rinse and repeat.

Jos: Rinse and repeat.

Both: Go back to the start and change the bathwater.

Vicky: The story of your life was never written
in newspapers.
It was written in bedsheets
and breakfasts. In Friday night
takeaways and Sunday dinners.
It can be rewritten again by you.
I know there were mornings when my feet couldn't make the slow,
small journey from bed to floor.
When my shoulders weren't capable of bearing
their own weight away from pillows.
For those days, I'm sorry.
Those are the days I trusted you to the warm rooms I'd prepared.
To the fullness
of the food cupboard and the fridge,
to computer rooms and TV screens,
to books and games and toys I'd bought for days like these.
The sudden absence of music stops me.
The clatter of metal on ceramic.
The door shifts, opens,
a waft of warm steam greets me.

Jos: A new face emerging.
Marked and scratched from slipping fingers,
But I'm smiling.

Vicky: He is smiling.

Scene 9

Jos: 2nd August 2018

Sometimes, when I was a bit younger, I used to get real jealous about kids who had their dads there. Especially the ones who liked doing stuff with 'em – football and cinema and fishing and that. But now, I don't feel the same anymore. I reckon I've got something else instead – something they won't have for a long time yet. So I've got a head start on them really. You see, all this has made me wanna try real hard to get what I want in life. It's made me realise that I'm strong. That nothing can knock me down. Not for long anyway.

Vicky: August 2018

I love coming here. My trolley is full of tuna and hummus and rich, red steak. I like to whizz in and out. I don't hang about 'cause I'm too busy. On top of Joseph and work and uni, I've got other shops I need to get to – like the home improvement places. Maybe they're my favourite now. Luckily for me, when I stopped holding up the sky,

Both: I discovered that my arms were strong.

Vicky: I had a knack for DIY.

Jos: The only way to make sure your foundations are firm is to build them yourself.

Vicky: My hands have cut, sawn and sanded new floorboards, laid tacks to hold carpets. Grouted in good, sturdy tiles. They've turned themselves to wiring too; chasing out loose connections, laying new trails, sparking new circuits.

Jos: I've sanded back to bare brick, begun again with brushes and bright white paint.

Vicky: People who come to visit sometimes find I make them linger too long on the doorstep, looking too closely at their feet before I let them in.

Both: You might catch me quietly checking and rechecking,

Vicky: feeling for the edges of the things you say,
tucking my questions tidily away.

Jos: Testing against the walls of things
to see if they crumble when I push.

Vicky: I'd like to see your skeleton,
check which way your bones
are inclined to bend.

Jos: I'm just trying to be cautious.

Vicky: Sometimes people have made a mess and it took a lifetime to get my floors clean.

Both: Promises and stories haven't always been my friends.

Vicky: So now I like to write them down. See them spread out on paper before I decide for sure if I'll put them away with my precious books on the shelves beside my desk. Presents from family and friends, they sit alongside photo albums, full up with the things I've decided I'd save.
There are days you'll find my office floor strewn with chopped up newspaper print.

Jos: I don't just accept them as they come. I like to get between the lines.

Vicky: I like to sew them back together with bits of stories I've written myself; if you mine beneath the shock of black on white, there are colours, tones, hues of light you might not expect to find there. Nowadays I can't always get what I need in the supermarket. For the soothing, scented bath salts, I'll go into town instead.

Jos: In the centre of town there's a car park.

Both: I've found it's the best place in the whole city to see the sky.

Jos: I like to go there at sunset.

Vicky: Watch the prelude to night .The wash of mauve and orange – how it dances towards darkness. I look out across the rooftops, to the river.

Both: Witness as she lets go of herself.

Vicky: Lets her water run out and reveals her scarred riverbed for a while; the marks left behind beneath the fullness, as she ebbs. When the light falls just right, the crevices fill with liquid gold, shine in the wetness.

Both: She's beautiful when you see her like that.

Joseph

1st January 2017

The day my life changed ... well, it was night actually. When my life changed,
I was sleeping. I used to have this blanket that I always took to bed; it was
blue fleece. Real soft. And this night, I had it in bed. And course, I was asleep.
'Cause I always used to sleep alright with that blanket. And so everything
that happened, happened while I was warm and cosy at home. And I didn't
know anything about it. Funny that, innit? How your life can change, and at
the time, you don't even know. And it was like my anchor, that blanket. You
could use it like a pair of arms, giving you a cuddle. It was like safety. And it
smelled like toast. It used to smell like toast.

I wish I knew where it began.
The seconds, the heartbeats that change everything.

I wonder how you make a man.
I wish I knew where it began.

His hands stacked wood and worked it to flame.
Passed exams that earned a uniform.
Lashed on breathing apparatus,
held maps, checked hydrants, broke down burning doors.

I wonder when they first held me.

15th January 2017

My mum's got boxes and boxes of stuff up in the loft – but she won't let
me in there. Sometimes she'll bring down some of my baby stuff; my first

baby-grow, the little tag thing you have on your arm when you're born, some photos. Like she'll only let me see the things she wants me to see. And I reckon she's saved every pair of shoes I ever owned. OK, maybe not every pair, but all the ones from when I was little. Maybe that's just what mums do...

Support
the bones of this boy;
vertebra, femur, fibula,
calcified foundations,
feet firmly held.

No dad has modelled the softness required of knuckles and wrist.

There must be a way to learn,
to grow the seed of personality,
pressed into fertility.
We wait to take flight.

The dad who would carry me home,
who would hold me,
shaking child.

Whispers I've heard:
what love can do for a person, what it can heal.
Wish for me. For a family. A home.

1st February 2017

When I was a real little kid, I used to love my little men. Used to take them everywhere – wrap them up in little bits of towels and fabric. I always wanted to keep them safe. Used to tuck them in at night. I remember once I lost them in the supermarket. My mum said I cried my eyes out, so she went back in and asked at the desk, to see if she could get them back....

Some things are irreplaceable;
his shoulders, his breath,
my footsteps,
headed across the landing,
trailing fingers along
the walls, singing.

Fragile weight.
We might all break.

Holding, pulling.

Lips moving
like a bad dream.
Like nothing's happened.
I can't cry.

He's gone.

3rd March 2017

I've still got my blue blanket. But I don't use it anymore. One day, I came home from school, and my mum had washed it, and it wasn't the same anymore. It smelled like fabric conditioner instead. And I know she meant well, but it didn't work anymore after that. So, I just keep it in a box under my bed now. With the photos. The ones from before that night. Before my life changed...

I'd have been all tucked up. Toys piled neatly in a corner while I slept. And I wish I hadn't asked. Almost wish I hadn't questioned.

There's a woman in a car park and someone's said it's him.

My head is spinning with things he's done, but nothing about the cool of ice-cream against lips and throat in the heat of a summer garden. Not that time you saved a little girl in a house fire. Laid her back against cold night pavement to bring her breath back.

Your face in the paper. Your face in the news. Everyone knows.

What does a three-year old know of prison? I'll tell you what he knows. Harry Potter. Azkaban. And then night terrors. My Daddy in a haunted castle.

Doubt is a prison cell.
He was a fireman.
He says he did not commit this cowardly act.
Cannot decide.

4th April 2017

Bath times are brilliant when you're a kid, aren't they? We used to have all these daft songs we'd sing – there was one for washing your armpits to, one for washing your hair, and one for afterwards when you were getting dry. We'd sing them real loud. Top of our voices. But I can't even think about that anymore. Don't know if I'm remembering it right or not...

All my boundaries have crumbled.
I need something solid...
All my stories are gone.
Nothing to hold onto.
The sight of other men's hands crooked to lift hair out of smiling eyes
is a physical pain.
I need clean white walls to block it out.

But sometimes white paint hides dark secrets,
words scratched in dirty brick.
Hands curved around a sharp object
can fracture everything.

Too much possibility.

It's not the kind of thing you hope for, is it?

29th April 2017

I loved primary school. I remember my first day - feeling real smart in my new school uniform, new school shoes, new bag. There was a toy fire engine in my classroom. I always wanted to play with it, and the teacher always used to make sure I'd get it at play times. She was nice like that. I think I must have been her favourite. And I remember my mum, smiling.

I remember her dropping me off. Waving from the classroom door.
I remember sunny days. I didn't see the shadows then.
You build up walls, but blood has a way of seeping through.
Hammers. Hammers.
Violent end for violent man.
Vicious revenge killing.
See him everywhere -
in my bedroom at night.
Lost father.
Father murdered.
Nowhere to go.
Cacophony, wearing down my brain.
Need my mum.
Need hot chocolates with marshmallows, carrot sticks, soft vanilla buns.

1st June 2017

She's never told me about that night. She thinks I'm too young. But I'm not daft. I know all about it. She thinks I don't, but I do. The kids at school don't let me forget it, 'cause they all know about it too. So why does she think I wouldn't? She thinks I'm daft. And there's loads of questions I want to ask. But I can't 'cause if I start talking about it, I can see her lip shaking. But I still wanna know. Like, do I walk like him? Do I talk like him? Is my body the same shape? I'm nearly grown now. So she must know …

Google is a bad dream
I can't wake up from -
the gristle of another man's ear
between my teeth.
I ache to make fists,
to find release in another man's face.
Sometimes, instead, fists find the wall.
Sometimes, instead, head finds the wall.
Sometimes, instead, I'll take a pill,
smoke some weed,
run away.
Soft hands bring me home.
Sit me down. Press my chest.
We crack our ribs
and hope they can help.
Really hope they can help.
These are not dead things.
They growl and screech.
They scratch and nip.
They do not lie still.

15th April 2018

They say these voices in my head are anxiety. Probably all these unanswered questions bouncing around and off each other. That's what I feel like I'm doing sometimes - bouncing around. Bouncing off walls. It's like somebody's taken my anchor away, and now I'm just floating about. There's too much space. Too much not knowing. And I don't know what to do. Don't know how to make it stop.

Clean-edged steel.
Scar-scattered arms.
Need to steady my hand,
need an arc to lean into.
I need bass, running water.
Don't know how to begin to...

My face in the mirror,
the blade in my hand.
Go steady. Fresh start.
A clean shave.

I send out wishes
        and hope
        and oaths ...
You do not have to grow where you land.
Rinse and repeat.
Go back to the start
and change the bathwater.

A new face emerging.
Marked and scratched from slipping fingers,
but I'm smiling.

2nd August 2018

Sometimes, when I was a bit younger, I used to get real jealous about kids who had their dads there. Especially the ones who liked doing stuff with em – football and cinema and fishing and that. But now, I don't feel the same anymore. I reckon I've got something else instead – something they won't have for a long time yet. So I've got a head start on them really. You see, all this has made me wanna try real hard to get what I want in life. It's made me realise that I'm strong. That nothing can knock me down. Not for long anyway.

I discovered that my arms were strong.
The only way to make sure your foundations are firm is to build them yourself.
I've sanded back to bare brick, begun again with brushes and bright white paint.

You might catch me quietly checking and rechecking,
testing against the walls of things
to see if they crumble when I push.
I'm just trying to be cautious;
promises and stories haven't always been my friends.
I don't just accept them as they come. I like to get between the lines.

In the centre of town, there's a car park.
I've found it's the best place in the whole city to see the sky.
I like to go there at sunset,
witness as she lets go of herself.
She's beautiful when you see her like that.

Me and DI Jones

There's about a foot between me and Sam as we perch on the edge of my bed. He looks up, catches my eye again - distracted from the busy work his hands are doing, and I hope I'm not blushing. Flirtation flashes blue sparks behind his eyes before he stamps them out; gets back to concentrating on the tangles between his fingers.

It would have been so much easier if we were doing this downstairs, or in any other room. But this is just one uncomfortable situation in a string that's been tying us together for a good while now. Things aren't helped by the fact that I still haven't unpacked properly, and even if I had, it wouldn't disguise the thinness of the carpet, the shoddily painted walls. He's about five years my senior – about the same age as the man he's here to protect me from – and under different circumstances it could be much more comfortable to be this close to him in a bedroom. If it had been a different man this might be easier. But it was Sam who'd knocked on my door three years ago and introduced himself as the undercover policeman that needed to speak to me about my ex.

Back then, we'd spent rather a lot of time together. He was full of hope about a long conviction and grateful for all my help. Now he only appeared each time I had to move house again. Each time he was perfectly polite, not commenting on the downward slip into more and more unsavoury areas.

'You sure I can't get you a cuppa?'

'Honestly, I'd better not. Need to get this sorted really.'

It didn't sting when he refused. Not like when some of the others did; they were accustomed to not drinking out of the dirty cups in the dirty houses of people in my sort of messy situation. I knew that wasn't the problem here, knew him well enough to know this wasn't about the state of my cups. Today he was in a rush. There was something going on that he hadn't told me about; couldn't tell me about yet. But it had infused urgency into the need to get my cameras and panic alarm working. I'd already been here a few weeks and I hadn't pestered them. Then he'd phoned this morning, flustered and worried, saying he needed to come and sort it. This hadn't worried me any more than usual - maybe the odd extra heartbeat in the seconds it took to get through the phone call. Panic had become a kind of dull overcoat I wore every day; I was too tired to bother taking it off and hanging it up every night. I knew I'd be putting it back on again. Its heavy, dragging heat had been slowing me down for a long time now. Maybe Sam thought my cups had got dirty in my cupboards after all. The kitchen they were in definitely wasn't the bright, clean, hopeful place I'd first brewed up in for him. Back then, pity wasn't the first thing I saw in his eyes when I met him – back then it was surprise.

'Aha. Got the fucking thing.'

I look up, and his thick blonde hair has fallen across his face, which is smiling. I try to smile back, but it's hard to muster any excitement. I clear a space on the windowsill where I know he wants the camera to be set up, overlooking my front path and the street beyond it. It's not a pretty picture they're going to catch; half the houses have metal screens across the windows, the rest hang with tatty curtains or broken blinds. Wind-blown wrappers are the only movement for now, but later, in darkness, the dealer across the road will attract his usual creeping custom. His little girl hangs on my gatepost again this morning. She should be at school.

'So when was the last time you actually saw him?'

I turn back into the room to answer, but I don't look him at him. The repetition of these questions has rubbed a sore spot in my head, and it's hard to concentrate.

'I didn't actually see him last time. There was an apple tree in a pot on the path, and a letter through the door when I got home from work two days ago.'

'What did it say?'

'Just the usual. It was for the boys – saying he misses them but I won't let them see him.'

'Well hopefully we'll be able to catch him on candid camera next time.'

'Hmm ... hopefully.'

I don't really see the point. They've been catching him on camera for months now, and it's made no difference. He's not supposed to come near us, but they don't seem to be able to stop him. I'm not going to ask what's happened to bring on this sudden rush, because I'm not sure I want to know – unless it's something that means he might be locked up again soon. That is the only thing that interests me now.

'Right then, I think we're good to go.'

Sam stands, with some of the straightened-out wires in his hands, and we set about fixing up the camera. When it's done, I thank him for coming, and as usual, he tells me to ring him if my ex turns up again. He's about to leave, but from the hallway he sees Joseph playing with his little men on the rug in the living room, and he hesitates.

'We're watching him, you know. We've got our eye on him. Any trouble at all, and you ring me.'

I stand at the door as he heads away down the path. I don't know where he's parked his car. Three years ago, when this was still a novelty, I used to joke that Sam moved in the shadows, slinking in and out of my house like a ninja. But it's not funny anymore. He's not a ninja, and this is not a film. If it was I wouldn't be in this house, on this street. I wouldn't still be scared every day; because in the films I watched, people who committed crimes served their time in prison – they didn't get out because of a lack of evidence and a convincing speech to the jury.

I'm relieved that Sam's gone. His expensive clothes and holiday tan have become more and more incongruous when he visits; the contentment that shows itself in his clear skin and his relaxed gait is out of place in my house now. It was an effort for him not to linger on the shadows around my eyes, the acne that has sprung up on my face. In the beginning he'd made the time to get to know me – chatting about music and the kids – we had a lot in common. He'd read all the police interviews, so he knew more about me than most people, but there was still a question that hovered between us unspoken when we met, like a sheet of film separating his life from mine. And now my own questions had thickened that film to a dividing wall. You could know facts and still not quite fathom truth, still not quite grasp how we'd ended up in that position today; the tangle of wires and posable police cameras spread between us, like the series of intertwining actions that had led us to be sitting on my bed together, a million miles apart.